THE
METAMORPHOSIS

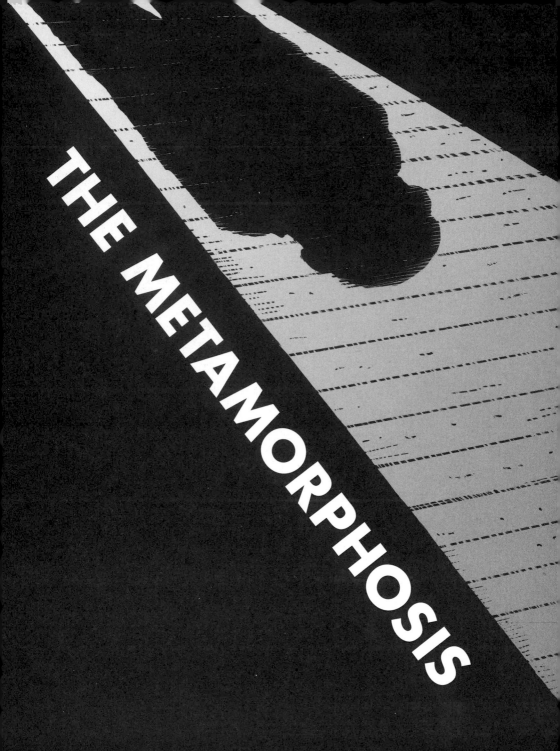

THE METAMORPHOSIS

FRANZ KAFKA

Dedicated to Gregor Samsas everywhere

THE INTRODUCTION

In 1904, more than a decade before Franz Kafka published *The Metamorphosis* in Prague, across the ocean a cartoonist named Winsor McCay created "Dream of the Rarebit Fiend," a comic strip that appeared in New York's *Evening Telegram*. In each one-page installment a character was trapped in a world that grew more surreal with each panel—a gentleman's leg inflates and demolishes a mansion, a suitor's lover crumbles into confetti and blows away, a lady's alligator handbag morphs into a monster and devours her. Finally, in the last panel, the character awakens to reality, vowing never again to eat the nightmare-inducing rarebit cheese before bedtime.

Of course, Franz Kafka never allowed his characters to enjoy the relief of awakening to normalcy from their disturbing dreams. Still, the two artists had much in common, including a shared genius for rendering the anxious intersection of reality and dreamscape. Kafka may never have been a comic strip fan, but his angst-ridden characters in reality-bending scenarios are ideally suited to this medium. This adaptation of *The Metamorphosis* couldn't exist without Kafka's illuminating words, but owes a visual debt to McCay's trailblazing excursions into the absurd darkness of slumberland. I have drawn tremendous inspiration from both these pioneers, fascinated by their ability to address our human condition with unexpected twists, brilliant artistry, and deadpan humor.

Nearly a century later, the works of Kafka and McCay seem as fresh as if they were created to reflect our current zeitgeist. Kafka's tales of nightmare trials and monolithic bureaucracies feel no more surreal than headlines from our daily newspapers. It makes one wish that simply avoiding rarebit cheese were the remedy.

—Peter Kuper

When Gregor Samsa
awoke one morning from
disturbing dreams,
he found himself
transformed . . .

11

12

13

14

15

The change in Gregor's voice must have been muffled by the wooden door because his mother was reassured and shuffled off. However, their little exchange made his father and sister aware that Gregor had not, as they assumed, left for work.

But Gregor had no intention of unlocking the door and felt thankful for the habit he had acquired as a traveling salesman of bolting it at night, even when he was at home.

Certain that the change in his voice was merely the first sign of a bad cold, Gregor decided to get up, get dressed, and most important, have a good breakfast.

First he tried to arise by moving the lower part of his body...

But this proved to be too sensitive.

Then he tried moving his upper body...

But then he feared if he fell, it would take a miracle not to injure his head.

Back where he started, he lay there expecting, perhaps, everything would simply return to normal.

19

21

23

Gregor knew if the manager left in this mood, it would seriously jeopardize his job.

I know I'm in a tight spot, but I'll work my way out...

Please sir, don't go just yet...

His parents didn't understand this, they were too preoccupied with their own immediate troubles.

HELP, FOR GOD'S SAKE, HELP!

Where was his sister, Grete? She could have detained the man. He'd have listened to her!

Gregor squeezed past his bedroom door and falling onto his many legs felt a physical well-being he hadn't felt all morning. With his feet firmly planted on the ground, he believed that final relief from all his bodily suffering was at hand.

II

By the time Gregor awoke from his coma-like sleep, it was dusk. Though he could see through a crack in the door that their pleasant apartment was not empty, all was silent.

As he lay there, Gregor thought about how proud he felt to have provided this comfortable home for his sister and parents.

Gregor was dismayed to find that not only was this food he normally loved repulsive to him, but his room with its high ceiling now made him quite nervous...

Though feeling slightly ashamed, Gregor scurried under his sofa. Despite the fact that his back was a little crushed and he was unable to raise his head, he felt immediately comforted, and there he spent the whole night.

And thus, Grete would feed Gregor twice a day.

Though Gregor had assumed his father had been left penniless after the collapse of his business five years earlier, he was pleased to hear otherwise.

He gathered that despite the disastrous crash, his father had managed to save a small sum of money. This was the first uplifting news Gregor had heard since his imprisonment.

Back when his father's business catastrophe had left the family in despair, Gregor had set to work with great earnestness and rose almost overnight from stock clerk...

...to traveling salesman.

And in no time was able to surprise and delight the family with his financial successes.

Those had been splendid times...

If only Gregor could have spoken to Grete and thanked her, he would have found it easier to accept all her help.

As it was, when she raced around tidying up, it oppressed him.

It's as though she were *suffocating!*

...Come, Mother, he's out of sight...

Are you certain this is a good idea?

Yes, Gregor needs more room to move around.

We can start with his dresser.

UMPH I'll pull, you push.

Careful. Don't strain yourself, dear.

UPH It's too heavy for us...

And doesn't this look...

Won't it look like we're showing Gregor we've given up all hope of him ever getting better?

Hearing his mother's words, Gregor realized that not a soul had spoken directly to him these last two months. He had been on the verge of forgetting his human past, but her voice brought him back to his senses...

Yes! The furniture must stay!

44

Mother— I'll fetch your medicine!

Grete, Let me Help

AHH!

SLAM!!

47

III

56

From that time on, much to Gregor's exasperation, this charwoman would crack open his door every morning and evening to get a peek at him...

Gregor grew so aggravated by these daily disturbances that early one morning as springtime neared, he turned on her as if to attack...

65

My dear parents!

SLAM!

Things can't go on like this!

We've done everything humanly possible to care for *it* and put up with *it!*

S-She's 100% right!

Cough, cough!

We must get rid of the notion that this—this *monster* is Gregor.

If he could understand us...

If this were Gregor, he'd have realized human beings couldn't live with such a *creature* and would have left voluntarily!

But this *animal* persecutes us, drives our roomers away—

The *only* solution is to get rid of him!

EEEK— He's at it again!!!

But Gregor had never intended to frighten anybody, most especially his sister.

He only wanted to crawl back to his room.

Granted, he did look peculiar in the attempt...

But his good intentions seemed to be recognized.

He was shocked by the distance and amazed that he had managed to traverse it in his condition.

AT LAST!

SLAM!

Soon he discovered that he could no longer move.
This didn't surprise him—it was more unnatural that he had
ever been able to crawl on those scrawny little legs...

And
now
what?

Though he felt pains throughout his body, they grew fainter and fainter.

Gregor thought of
his family with
tenderness and love...

And with a certainty
possibly stronger
than his sister's,
he knew he had
to disappear.

He lay in a state
of empty and
peaceful reflection
until the clock tower
struck 3 A.M.

After all they had been through, the family needed a well-deserved rest, so they decided to take the day off and wrote letters of excuse to their employers...

Well, I've finished up...

and...

And what?

and...

You don't have to worry about getting rid of that thing.

I've disposed of the old dung b—

ENOUGH!!

Humph! Well, I'm in a rush anyway so...

SLAM!

We'll fire her tonight!

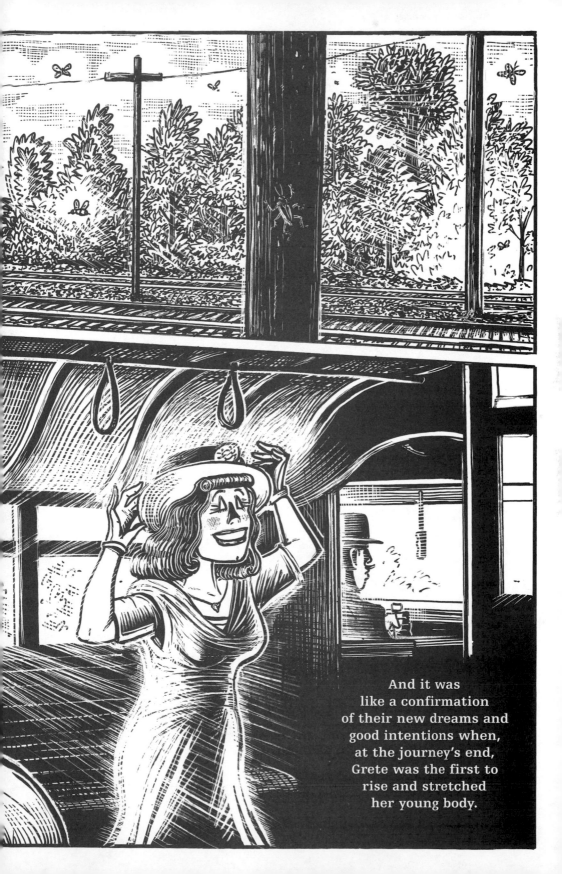

And it was
like a confirmation
of their new dreams and
good intentions when,
at the journey's end,
Grete was the first to
rise and stretched
her young body.

ABOUT THE ARTIST

PETER KUPER was born in 1958 and grew up in Cleveland, Ohio. He moved to New York City in 1977 and attended Pratt Institute in Brooklyn. Peter is cofounder of the political magazine *World War 3 Illustrated,* which he has coedited over the last 23 years, and has taught courses in comics at the School of Visual Arts since 1986. He has written and illustrated numerous graphic novels, including *Give It Up!,* his first collection of Franz Kafka adaptations, *The System, Eye of the Beholder, Stripped,* and *Comics Trips,* which chronicles an eight-month trip through Africa and Southeast Asia. His previous book, *Speechless,* is a career retrospective.

Peter's illustrations appear regularly in many magazines and newspapers, including *Time,* the *New York Times,* and *MAD,* for which he draws *Spy Vs. Spy* every month. His work can be seen on the Web at www.peterkuper.com.

ACKNOWLEDGMENTS

Thanks and appreciation to a great number of people
who helped bring this project to light:

my beautiful wife, Betty Russell,
for all her marvelous suggestions and eternal patience;

Steve Ross, my longtime friend,
and Chris Jackson, my diligent editor, at Crown;

Terry Nantier at NBM for years of support;

Ryan Inzana for his endless assistance;

John Thomas for lending his legal expertise;

Emily Russell for her fantastic editorial eye;

Kerstin Hasenpusch for a fine job of translating;

Susy Bernstein for her scholarly perspective;

Gahan Wilson, Will Eisner, and Jules Feiffer
for their ongoing encouragement;

my ever supportive family;

my friends Tony, Molly, Philip, Scott, Elena, and Seth;

and especially my daughter, Emily, for "bug book" enthusiasms.

Finally, thanks to Franz Kafka, who was kind enough to put
pen to paper in the first place and create a masterpiece